Lana Lynn and the New Watchdog

To the Brandt Flock
Ewe all keep me in stitches!
—R. V. S.

To my Bridgetown group, the ones that keep me grounded
—A. S.

Published by
PEACHTREE PUBLISHING COMPANY INC.
1700 Chattahoochee Avenue
Atlanta, Georgia 30318-2112
www.peachtree-online.com

Edited by Kathy Landwehr
Design and composition by Adela Pons

The illustrations were rendered digitally

Printed in March 2021 by Leo Paper Group in China
10 9 8 7 6 5 4 3 2 1
First Edition
ISBN 978-1-68263-196-6

Cataloging-in-Publication Data is available from the Library of Congress.

Lana Lynn and the New Watchdog

Written by Rebecca Van Slyke
Illustrated by Anca Sandu

PEACHTREE
ATLANTA

Lana Lynn was an intrepid sheep.

She loved running through the wild woods at night.

She loved staying up late.

She loved howling at the moon.

One morning, as she returned to the meadow, the flock was in an uproar.

"Have you heard?" her friend Shawn called. "We're getting a watchdog to guard the flock!"

"Golly, gee! I hope he's a good watchdog," Lana Lynn said. "I hear there are wolves in these woods." She looked at Shawn. "He'll probably need us to train him."

That very afternoon a stranger with yellow eyes and pointed teeth crept out of the wild woods.

Lana Lynn bounded up to him. “I know who you are!” she said. “You’re here to watch the sheep.”

The stranger nodded.

“Golly, gee! I knew it!” shouted Lana Lynn. “Get ready for Watchdog Lessons!”

She pushed the new watchdog over to Shawn. “Our new watchdog is here!” she shouted.

Shawn looked at the new watchdog’s yellow eyes and pointed teeth. “Are you sure he’s the new watchdog, Lana Lynn?”

Lana Lynn turned to the newcomer. "You're here to take care of the sheep, aren't you?"

The stranger licked his lips and nodded.

"See?" said Lana Lynn to Shawn.

She looked at the newcomer. "Fiddle-dee-dee! Now don't be nervous. I'll train you," she said.

Lana Lynn and Shawn took the new watchdog to the top of the hill. They looked at the flock grazing in the meadow.

"Lesson One," said Lana Lynn. "A good watchdog has to make sure that the flock has grass to nibble and water to drink. Why don't you try moving them from the meadow to the pond?" She gave him a push toward the sheep.

The sheep scattered as the new watchdog ran after them.

“Move them to the pond!” Lana Lynn shouted.

“Keep them together!”

"There are some
over there!"

"That one's getting away!
Now run over there!"

Shawn looked at Lana Lynn.
"Run faster!" he shouted.
"You can do it!"

Lana Lynn and Shawn cheered on the new watchdog all afternoon.

But by sunset, the flock
had yet to reach the pond.

“Fiddle-dee-dee! Don’t give up now! It’s time for our next lesson,” said Lana Lynn.

"Lesson Two: Watchdogs must always be on guard, day and night. You never know when a wolf or a coyote is around."

All night long, and all the next day,
Lana Lynn and Shawn took turns
keeping the new watchdog awake.

By evening, the new watchdog
was exhausted.

"Fiddle-dee-dee!" Lana Lynn said. "Don't give up now! There's SO much more for you to learn!"

They propped up the new watchdog, and Lana Lynn continued. "Lesson Three: Watchdogs must protect the flock from danger. Get ready to save Shawn!"

Lana Lynn put on her special gray blanket and gave a long, loud howl. She stalked toward Shawn. “Now pick up Shawn and save him,” she said.

The new watchdog grabbed Shawn.
"Uh, Lana Lynn?" said Shawn.

Lana Lynn gave her fiercest growl and her loudest howl. “Lessons are over,” she said. “Put Shawn down now.”

Lana Lynn watched the new watchdog as he ran down the hill and out of sight. "Fiddle-dee-dee," she said to Shawn. "That new watchdog wasn't very brave at all."

When they joined the rest of the flock in the meadow, the sheep were gathered around a new arrival. She had soft brown eyes and floppy ears.

"Golly, gee! *You* must be our new watchdog," said Lana Lynn. "You're pretty small. But don't worry. I'll train you."

"Fiddle-dee-dee," said Shawn.

Now the flock is guarded by a real watchdog…

…and her intrepid friend, Lana Lynn.